A Note to Parents and Caregivers:

Read-it! Readers are for children who are just starting on the amazing road to reading. These beautiful books support both the acquisition of reading skills and the love of books.

 The PURPLE LEVEL presents basic topics and objects using high frequency words and simple language patterns.

 The RED LEVEL presents familiar topics using common words and repeating sentence patterns.

 The BLUE LEVEL presents new ideas using a larger vocabulary and varied sentence structure.

 The YELLOW LEVEL presents more challenging ideas, a broad vocabulary, and wide variety in sentence structure.

 The GREEN LEVEL presents more complex ideas, an extended vocabulary range, and expanded language structures.

 The ORANGE LEVEL presents a wide range of ideas and concepts using challenging vocabulary and complex language structures.

When sharing a book with your child, read in short stretches, pausing often to talk about the pictures. Have your child turn the pages and point to the pictures and familiar words. And be sure to reread favorite stories or parts of stories.

There is no right or wrong way to share books with children. Find time to read with your child, and pass on the legacy of literacy.

Adria F. Klein, Ph.D.
Professor Emeritus
California State University
San Bernardino, California

Editor: Christianne Jones
Page Production: Zachary Trover
Creative Director: Keith Griffin
Editorial Director: Carol Jones
Managing Editor: Catherine Neitge
The illustrations in this book were created with watercolor paint and ink.

Picture Window Books
5115 Excelsior Boulevard
Suite 232
Minneapolis, MN 55416
877-845-8392
www.picturewindowbooks.com

Printed in the United States of America.

Library of Congress Cataloging-in-Publication Data
Dahl, Michael.
What's bugging Pamela? / by Michael Dahl ; illustrated by Zachary Trover.
p. cm. — (Read-it! readers)
Summary: Pamela the rhinoceros is always angry until a strange bird lands on her back
and refuses to leave.
ISBN 1-4048-1189-3 (hard cover)
[1. Rhinoceroses—Fiction.] I. Title: What is bugging Pamela? II. Trover, Zachary, ill.
III. Title. IV. Series.

PZ7.D15134Wha 2005
[E]—dc22
                                                            2005003902

What's Bugging Pamela?

by Michael Dahl
illustrated by Zachary Trover

Special thanks to our advisers for their expertise:

Adria F. Klein, Ph.D.
Professor Emeritus, California State University
San Bernardino, California

Susan Kesselring, M.A.
Literacy Educator
Rosemount–Apple Valley–Eagan (Minnesota) School District

PiCTURE WiNDOW BOOKS
Minneapolis, Minnesota

Pamela never smiled. Everything made her angry. Everything bugged her.

Early in the morning,
Pamela got mad at
the sun.

"It's too bright," said Pamela.

When she waded into the river,
she got mad at the water.

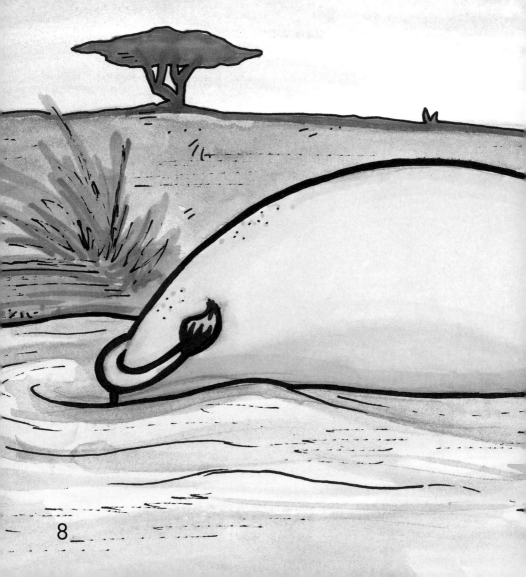

"It's too wet," said Pamela.

In the afternoon, Pamela's friends asked her to play.

"Why would I want to play with you?" said Pamela.

11

Pamela's friends talked
about her.

"She is always so mad," they said. "Pamela is a crabby sort of animal."

After a while, Pamela's friends
stopped asking her to play.

"I knew they didn't like me,"
said Pamela.

At night, the monkeys chattered in the trees. Pamela shouted at them.

"Be quiet!" she yelled. "Some animals are trying to sleep."

One day, Pamela got a surprise.

A strange bird landed on her back.

"Get off my back!" yelled Pamela. "You're bugging me!"

The bird said nothing.

"You're too heavy!" shouted
Pamela. "Go away."

The bird did not fly away. Then,
Pamela got another surprise.

The bird started
pecking at
Pamela's back.

"Stop it!" yelled Pamela. "Leave me alone."

Peck! Peck! Peck! Pamela started to feel different.

The bird was eating small bugs
that crawled on Pamela's back.

The bugs had been
making Pamela feel itchy
and angry all the time!

"Thank you," said the bird. "Those bugs tasted wonderful."

"Thank you," said Pamela. "I feel so much better now."

Then, a strange thing happened ...

Pamela smiled!

More *Read-it!* Readers

Bright pictures and fun stories help you practice your reading skills. Look for more books at your level.

At the Beach by Patricia M. Stockland
The Bossy Rooster by Margaret Nash
Dust Bunnies by Michael Dahl
Frog Pajama Party by Michael Dahl
Jack's Party by Ann Bryant
The Playground Snake by Brian Moses
Recycled! by Jillian Powell
The Sassy Monkey by Anne Cassidy

Looking for a specific title or level? A complete list of *Read-it!* Readers is available on our Web site:
www.picturewindowbooks.com